P9-EME-508

The Code of the Drum

L.L. Owens
AR B.L.: 3.0
Points: 0.5   MG

T 31008

B

The Code of the Drum

by L. L. Owens

Perfection Learning®

Cover Design: Alan D. Stanley
Inside and Cover Illustration: Margaret Sanfilippo

About the Author

Lisa L. Owens grew up in the Midwest. She studied English and journalism at the University of Iowa. Currently, she works as an editor and freelance writer in Seattle.

Other Civil War books by Ms. Owens include *Abraham Lincoln: A Great American Life*, *America's Civil War*, and *Brothers at War*.

Image credits: Tria Giovan/Corbis front cover (background image)

Art Today pp. 1, 2, 4, 5, 7, 8, 9, 10, 11, 15, 16, 17, 18, 19, 21, 22, 23, 25, 27, 28, 35, 37, 39, 40, 41, 42, 45, 49, 50, 51, 52, 54, 55, 56; Library of Congress pp. front cover, 24, 34, 43, 53; Digital Stock pp. 29, 30–31

Text © 2000 Perfection Learning® Corporation.
All rights reserved. No part of this book may be used or reproduced in any manner whatsoever without written permission from the publisher. Printed in the United States of America. For information, contact Perfection Learning® Corporation, 1000 North Second Avenue, P.O. Box 500, Logan, Iowa 51546-0500.
Phone: 1-800-831-4190 • Fax: 1-712-644-2392
Paperback ISBN 0-7891-5310-6
Cover Craft® ISBN 0-7807-9654-3

Contents

Chapter 1

News from the War

Jacob McCoy ran to the door. He greeted his grandfather.

"Hi, Grandfather!" he said. "What all did you get at the general store?"

Grandfather didn't answer. He looked serious. But Jacob didn't notice. He also didn't notice that Grandfather hadn't brought any **goods** inside. All he carried was a single letter in a fancy envelope.

"Where's your mother?" Grandfather asked.

"She's in the back room," said Jacob. "Did her new curtain fabric come in? She's been waiting for it for weeks."

Grandfather placed a hand on Jacob's shoulder. "Why don't you go outside? Play for a while," he said.

"I can't," Jacob replied. "Mama asked me to tend to the fire. Then I'm to set the table for supper."

"Go ahead, Jacob," Grandfather said. "It will be okay. I'll tell your mother. Just be back in time to eat."

"Thanks, Grandfather!" Jacob exclaimed. He hurried outside to look for his friends.

Jacob's mother entered the room. "Back so soon, Pa?" Mama asked. "I thought you were picking up a full load of goods today."

"I picked up the mail first," he said. "I decided to bring this straight home. It's from Captain Wagner." He handed the envelope to his daughter.

"That's James's commanding officer," said Mama. She looked at her father. "Oh, Pa!" she cried.

She tore into the envelope and read the letter quickly. It was just as she'd feared. Her husband was a **Union** soldier. And he had died.

"What's happened to James?" Grandfather asked. "Has he been hurt?"

"No," Mama said. "He's dead. He died two weeks ago from **typhoid fever**."

Grandfather put his arms around his daughter. "I am so sorry, dear," he said.

Mama cried softly for a few moments. Then she thought of her son. She wiped her eyes and asked, "Where's Jacob?"

"I sent him out to play," Grandfather said. "I thought this might be bad news. Jacob will be back for supper. We'll tell him then."

"This is going to be so hard on him," Mama said.

Grandfather sighed, "I know."

Chapter 2

Papa's Letters

Each night for the next week, Jacob went to his room right after supper. The news of Papa's death had left him sad and confused. He didn't feel much like talking or playing.

One night, he pulled out a little wooden box. It was filled with old letters. Most of them were from Papa.

Papa used to write to him every week. He told Jacob about the battles he fought in. He wrote about life in the camp. And he wrote about traveling with the troops.

Papa had been away for two years. I've missed him so much, Jacob thought. Now he's gone forever.

Jacob read a letter dated July 21, 1861.

July 21, 1861

Dear Jacob,

We traveled 13 miles today. That was a long march. I'm in the **infantry**. So I carry all my things on my back. (Wagons carry the officers' things.)

It was so hot today. My pack weighs about 30 pounds. It seemed like 100 pounds!

We set up camp along the river at sundown. I'm writing to you just outside the tent by the campfire. It helps keep the mosquitoes away. Sort of.

I share the tent with Robert. He's our drummer. He helped pick out the drum I sent you.

Robert and I forgot our tent poles at the last camp. We set up the tent tonight using our muskets instead. You would laugh if you saw it.

We think we can buy new poles from the **sutler**. I bought my writing kit from him. I bought my "housewife" from him too. (That's what we call our sewing kits.)

I've settled into the routine of being a soldier. It's tough. But it can also be boring. There's lots of waiting. We pass the time by playing games.

We play checkers and dominoes. Robert has a pocket-size chess set that we use. And there's always a poker game going on somewhere in the camp.

By the way—thank you for the picture of you, your mother, and Grandfather. I look at it every night. I show it to others when I tell stories about you. That's the main thing we do to pass the time here. We talk about home.

I'll write again next week.

With love,
Papa

Carefully, Jacob folded the letter. He put it back into the box. He reached for another.

Reading his father's words helped Jacob feel better. It was almost as if Papa were speaking to him.

January 5, 1863

Dear Jacob,

I just finished a letter to your mother. Now it's time to say hello to my boy!

Your mother says that you're getting taller all the time. I suppose I won't know you when I get home. It looks like that won't be for a while, though. This war just keeps going.

You said in your last letter that you've been taking drumming lessons. Do you like to play? Grandfather says you're pretty good.

I think of you now every time our drummer beats a drum call. The drum calls tell us what to do. We hear them all day long in camp.

The drummer plays **reveille** when it's time to get up in the morning. He issues other calls too. When it's time to eat. When it's time for a drill. And even when it's time for bed.

He helps us while we march and during battles too. His drum calls are like a code. I wish you could hear them. But I'm glad you're safe at home.

It's time for me to go. Say hi to Grandfather.

All my love,
Papa

Jacob gazed at his drum in the corner of his room. He imagined himself drumming calls to Union troops.

Suddenly, he had an idea!

Chapter 3

Jacob's Plan

"Absolutely not!" Mama exclaimed.

"We won't allow it!" said Grandfather.

"Papa would let me join his old **regiment**," said Jacob. "He'd want me to. I just know it."

"No, he wouldn't," Mama replied sternly. "He would never let his 12-year-old son join the army."

"I'm 13," said Jacob.

"Not till next month," Grandfather reminded him. "You've got no cause to join the fighting."

"But Papa's regiment lost several men to the fever. They need help. And I can give it to them."

"They can **recruit** new men," Mama said. "Grown-up men."

"Plenty of boys my age have gone to war," Jacob said. "I know you've heard about them. Remember that newspaper article? It said lots of buglers and drummers are boys. That way the men can stick to the fighting."

"I know that you want to do something to honor your father," Mama said. "And I understand that you want to help the Union. But I won't hear of it. Besides, you're in school now. And I don't want you to miss it. Your father wouldn't either."

"Papa left school when he was 11," Jacob said. "He did fine."

"Your father had no choice," Grandfather replied. "He had to quit school. He had to help support his family. Your father worked hard. Because of that, you are able to go to school. Until you finish. *That's* what your father wanted for you."

"Things are different now," Jacob said. "The Civil War has changed everything. Papa wanted to help the Union. And I do too. It's more important right now than me going to school."

"Not to me, Jacob," Mama said. "The matter is settled. You're going to stay put and finish school. You can join the army when you're older."

Jacob sulked for the rest of the evening. He went to bed early.

Jacob awoke with a start. It was the middle of the night. He'd dreamed about his father. Papa had called out to him. He'd asked Jacob to join him. The steady beat of a drum had sounded in the distance.

Jacob made a decision.

I know Papa would understand, Jacob thought. I just hope Mama and Grandfather do.

Chapter 4

On the Run

Jacob rode across the countryside. He thought about Mama and Grandfather. He hoped that they were okay. He had left them a note. It read

Dear Mama and Grandfather,
When you read this, I will be gone. I plan to find Papa's regiment. Papa said where they were in his letters. I'm going to see if they'll let me be a drummer.
Please don't worry. I'll write to you when I get to the camp.

Love,
Jacob

Jacob had been riding now for eight days. He usually rode from sunup to sundown. He expected to reach his 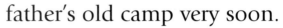father's old camp very soon.

Late that afternoon, his horse was jumpy. He seemed almost afraid.

The air was thick. Jacob thought he smelled smoke. But he didn't see a camp. He didn't even see a town nearby. He slowed down a little when he came to an open field.

"Whoa, boy. What is it?" Jacob's horse whinnied and pranced.

Jacob stopped. He took in the scene. There were patches of burnt grass. There were bloodied scraps of soldiers' uniforms. There were bullets and shattered pieces of weapons. There were bits of boots and hats. And there were a few dead horses.

"It's a battlefield!" exclaimed Jacob. He patted his horse. "Looks like we came at the right time, boy. This battle's over!"

Jacob explored the field for a while. They've already cleared the field of the dead and wounded, he thought. That means that they've moved on.

Jacob moved on too. Eventually he crossed a river. This looks like a good place to stop for the night, he thought. He tied up the horse near the water. And he went for a walk in the woods.

Soon Jacob heard voices.

I must be near a camp, Jacob thought. He made his way through the trees to a clearing. Sure enough, there was a small army camp. But which army was it? Was it Union or **Confederate**?

Jacob climbed a big tree at the edge of camp. He had a clear view of the grounds. A flag hung in the middle of camp. It had two red stripes, one white stripe, and seven stars on a blue border in the left corner.

The Stars and Bars, Jacob thought. They're Confederates!

Just then, a drummer appeared from a tent below. A second one followed. They were about 20 feet from Jacob. But they had no idea that he was overhead.

"Okay," said the first one. "Teach me the new Safe Passage call."

The second drummer rattled off the call. The first drummer tried it. He missed some of the strokes.

"No. You missed this part," said the second drummer. He played it again. "That's the code. It's how you can tell this call from the one Union drummers use. You have to get it right. If you try to pass by another Confederate camp at night and you get it wrong . . ." he shook his head. "The guards will start shooting! Before you even get a chance to correct your mistake. Then your whole regiment will be in danger."

The first drummer tried again. And again, he missed the most important part.

Jacob watched as the second drummer played it over and over. Finally, the first drummer joined in. That time he got it right. On his leg, Jacob tapped out the rhythm right along with them.

Then the drummers called the other soldiers to supper. Jacob hurried back to his horse.

I'd better keep moving tonight. At least for a while, he thought. He wanted to get closer to the Union camp. And he wanted to move far away from the Confederate camp.

The beat of the Safe Passage call echoed in his mind as he rode.

Chapter 5

Jacob Finds the Union Camp

The next morning, Jacob approached another camp. This one was out in the open. The guards could see him.

Jacob saw the Stars and Stripes. It was a Union flag. He was relieved. He'd reached his father's Union camp at last.

He rode up to one of the guards. He asked, "Can you tell me where to find Captain Wagner of the 33rd Infantry?"

The guard asked, "What's your business, son?"

"I'd like to join up," Jacob replied.

The guard laughed. Many young boys found their way to the army camps. They all wanted to join the fighting.

"Captain Wagner's tent is at the back of the camp. It's one of the big ones. You can't miss it."

Jacob hesitated. He wasn't sure what to do.

"Go on in, son," urged the guard. "You'd better go. At least while I'm still in the mood to let you!"

Jacob rode to the end of a long line of canvas tents. He tied up his horse and looked around. Soon he saw what had to be Captain Wagner's tent. It was twice the size of the others.

Jacob peered inside. He saw a bed, a huge trunk, a small table with two chairs, a writing desk, a sword—

"What do you want?" a deep voice demanded.

Jacob was startled. He whirled around.
"I–I–I'm looking for Captain Wagner," he said.

"You've found him," the captain said
gruffly. He puffed on his pipe. "Do I know
you?"

"No, sir," Jacob replied. "But you knew my
father. James McCoy."

The captain's face softened. "I see. What's
your name, son?"

"Jacob. Jacob McCoy."

"Glad to meet you, Jacob McCoy. What brings you here?" the captain asked.

"I heard that you've lost many men," Jacob said. "I want to join up."

"How old are you?" asked Captain Wagner.

"I'm 13," said Jacob. "Almost."

"We do need extra men," said the captain. "However, 'almost 13' is quite young. Does your mother know you're here?"

"Yes," said Jacob. It was the truth. He didn't mention one thing, though. She had forbidden him to leave home.

"Well," Captain Wagner said, "I don't think—"

"But I'm a drummer!" Jacob interrupted. He didn't give the captain a chance to turn him down. "I'm really good! You'll see!"

Jacob dashed over to his horse. Then he dashed back with his drum. "Let me play for you," he said. He tapped out a hard rhythm.

Captain Wagner said, "That's nice, Jacob. But we need someone to beat the army drum calls."

"I already know reveille," Jacob said. "And I'm a fast learner. Honest."

He played reveille for the captain. His strokes were sharp and clear. The captain was impressed.

A soldier stuck his head out of his tent. "Hey!" he shouted. "Some of us are trying to catch a nap. You shouldn't go playing reveille. Not unless it's daybreak!"

"Calm down, Tom," said Captain Wagner. "This is James McCoy's son. He was just showing me what he can do. What do you think?"

"He sounds good," Tom said. "We could use a drummer to take Robert's place."

"That's right," said Captain Wagner. "Robert went home."

"Robert? Pa's friend?" Jacob asked.

"Yes," Tom said. "He was hurt in our last scuffle. He lost an arm."

"So you really *do* need me," Jacob said to Captain Wagner.

"Didn't you hear what Tom said?" the captain replied. "It's dangerous on the battlefield. Johnny Reb doesn't care if you're a drummer. Or a young boy. You could be hurt. You could even die."

"I want to help the Union any way I can," Jacob said. "For Papa."

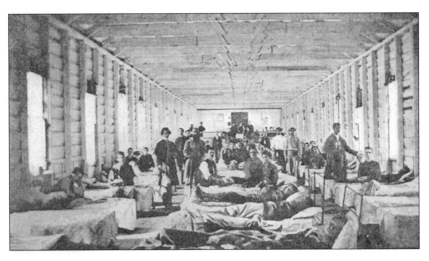

Captain Wagner studied Jacob's face. "Okay, Jacob," he said. "You're in. Tom can help you get settled. We'll use your horse to help pull the wagons."

He went on. "Hank, the bugler, and Charles, the fife player, can teach you the drum calls. You'll need to know them by next week. *All of them.* Understood?"

"I can do it, sir," Jacob promised.

"I hope I don't regret this decision," said Captain Wagner. Then, with a wave, he turned and disappeared into his tent.

"Catch!" Tom said. He tossed a worn **haversack** to Jacob.

Jacob caught it. He looked at the name tag sewn inside. It said

James McCoy, 33rd Infantry

"This was Papa's!" Jacob gasped.

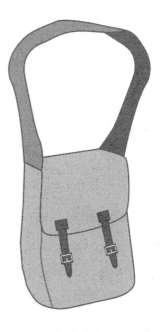

Tom said, "Thought you might want it. We already divided up the things other soldiers could use. Like his clothes and bedroll. But we planned to send that to his family. Since you're here . . ."

"Thank you," Jacob said.

"You bet, kid," said Tom.

Jacob eagerly searched the bag. He found a knife, fork, and spoon set. There was a wooden canteen and a tin cup. A toothbrush and a comb were stuck next to a shaving set, a sewing kit, and a writing set. There was a deck of cards. And there was the family photo James had loved.

"Here are your rations," Tom said. He gave Jacob some salted meat, dried vegetables, hardtack, and coffee. "Keep 'em in your haversack."

Later that night, Jacob pulled out his father's writing set. He wrote by the light of the fire.

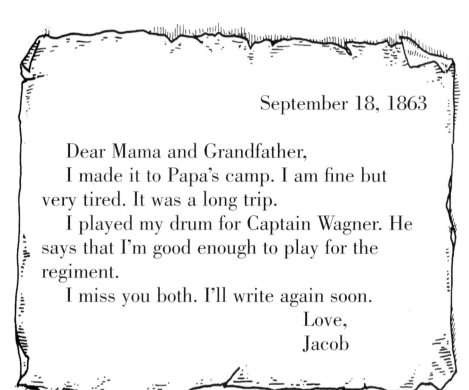

September 18, 1863

Dear Mama and Grandfather,
I made it to Papa's camp. I am fine but very tired. It was a long trip.
I played my drum for Captain Wagner. He says that I'm good enough to play for the regiment.
I miss you both. I'll write again soon.
Love,
Jacob

Chapter 6

The New Drummer Boy

Jacob trained hard the next week. Hank and Charles taught him all the drum calls. They also gave him a copy of the army's songbook to learn.

When he wasn't practicing the calls, Jacob did chores around camp. He carried water and delivered messages. He helped the wounded men. He mended officers' uniforms. He served food. He even cut a few men's hair!

It was just before dawn on Sunday. Charles shook Jacob awake. "Test time," Charles said.

"What test?" asked Jacob. He rubbed his eyes.

"The one where we see how much you've learned," said Hank. "Come on. Get your drum and your sticks. You're the drummer boy now. And you've got work to do."

Jacob followed Hank and Charles outside.

"Play reveille," said Hank.

"Aren't you going to play your bugle?" Jacob asked.

"Nope," Hank replied. "It's your turn."

"Let's hear it," said Charles.

Jacob played reveille loud and clear as the sun came up. He watched the camp come to life.

Next Charles said, "Call them to breakfast." And Jacob did. His drumming was perfect.

Jacob spent the rest of the day issuing official drum calls. He announced an inspection. He called everyone to church, then to lunch. He signaled the start of an officers' meeting. And during a march, his playing told the troops which way to turn— and when.

After supper, Captain Wagner found Jacob. He slapped Jacob on the back. He said, "You're doing a good job, son. Keep it up."

Chapter 7

Marching Orders

Jacob issued the Foot March call. He and the rest of the troops had packed up camp. They were marching out. It was after dark.

He looked back at the now-empty clearing. He saw a few smoldering campfires. They were the only signs that there had been a camp.

Captain Wagner had received a message from a Union spy. A Confederate unit was planning to attack their camp soon.

The captain decided to move toward the enemy first. He wanted to take them by surprise.

Jacob marched next to Captain Wagner. Jacob's drum beat kept the soldiers moving at a brisk pace.

The captain told Jacob his orders for the troops. Jacob would then play the code. The troops followed whatever instructions the drum called out.

As he marched, Jacob realized something. They were heading for the Rebel camp he'd seen on his trip!

They marched all night. Eventually, Captain Wagner ordered Jacob to stop playing. "We're getting close," he said. "We don't want to announce our arrival!"

Hundreds of men marched in time—without a beat. The steady crunch of their footsteps was muffled in the night air.

Soon they were close enough to see the Confederate camp. Many campfires lit up the area. Officers were shouting orders. And soldiers bustled about.

Captain Wagner's troops came to a stop just outside the Confederate guards' field of vision. Luckily, the light from the camp made it easy for Captain Wagner to see the five guards.

"What's going on?" Jacob asked. "Why aren't they sleeping?"

"They're preparing for battle," answered Captain Wagner. "Looks like they plan to move toward our camp at dawn. If we act quickly—and quietly—we can get by the guards. Then we can enter the camp from the other side. They'll never know what hit 'em!"

Chapter 8

Safe Passage

Jacob tapped his drumsticks together. This signaled the first line of troops to move forward. The rest fell in line.

They slipped by the first three guards unnoticed. The activity in camp masked the noise of the Union's movement.

The fourth guard thought he heard something. He couldn't see anything, though. He decided that his mind was playing tricks on him.

Moments later, the Union troops were almost past the fifth guard. The plan was working.

Jacob was excited. He turned to Captain Wagner. He was about to whisper a question. But Jacob stepped on a rock. He tripped out of step. His hand hit the drum. And his sticks hit the rim.

The fifth guard heard that for sure. He moved toward the trees. He raised his gun and alerted the other guards.

Captain Wagner ordered the troops to keep moving in silence. The battle was going to begin a bit sooner than planned.

Jacob's mind raced. "The Rebs know we're here. It's all my fault," he thought. Then it hit him.

"Captain Wagner, sir!" he whispered. "I know the Confederate Safe Passage code. It might buy us some time."

"That's enough, Jacob," said the captain. He hadn't yet heard of this code. And he didn't trust Jacob right now.

Jacob took a chance anyway. He played the Safe Passage. He remembered it!

The guards recognized the code. "They're Confederates too," one said to another. "Let them pass." All five relaxed.

This was just the opportunity Jacob's regiment needed. By the time the guards saw that they were Union soldiers, it was too late. They had missed their chance to warn the camp.

The guards were easily captured. So were the rest of the surprised Confederate soldiers!

The Union marched out a few hours later with their prisoners. They sang "The Battle Hymn of the Republic," "Polly Wolly Doodle," and several other lively tunes.

Finally, the singing stopped. Captain Wagner told Jacob to play a rousing Union march.

"Play it as loud as you want!" said the captain. "This is our territory now. Thanks to your quick thinking. You've done your father proud."

With that, Jacob broke into his favorite marching beat. And he played it as loudly as he could manage.

Civil War Drum Calls

Assembly
Troops fell in for roll call when this was played. Then they loaded baggage on the wagon.

Chammade
This sounded a wish to speak to the enemy.

Church
This summoned the soldiers to church.

Drummer
This beat gathered the drummers.

Foot March
This told the soldiers to march.

Long Roll

This continuous drumming told the regiment to assemble.

Memento Mori

This is Latin for "I remember the dead."

Preparative

This told the soldiers to get ready to fire.

Retreat

This was beat at sunset to tell the soldiers to come into camp before the gates were shut.

Reveille

This call awakened the camp at daybreak. It also told the guards that their shift was finished. Drummers could beat reveille. But it was often called by bugles.

Rogue's March

This was beaten on drums and played by the fifes. It was used when a soldier was drummed out of (sent away from) the regiment.

Sergeant

This called the sergeants together.

Tap-Too

This was a long period of continuous drumming. It told soldiers to retire to their quarters at night. It also signaled that no more liquor could be sold. It was rarely beat in camp.

To Arms

This immediately summoned soldiers to their alarm posts.

Troop

See Assembly.

Glossary

Confederate   another name for the Southern states. The soldiers were often called Rebels or Johnny Rebs.

goods   supplies

haversack   small canvas sack. Soldiers carried food in it.

infantry   soldiers trained to fight on foot

recruit	enlist or increase the number of
regiment	military unit of men
reveille	call to awaken the camp at daybreak; usually sounded by a bugle or drum
sutler	person who sold things that soldiers needed. He was not a member of the army.

typhoid fever

contagious disease caused by bacteria. High fever, headache, diarrhea, and death are common.

Union

another name for the United States. The soldiers were often called Yankees or Yanks.

9014